A Beginning-to-Read Book

W9-AZZ-239

What's in the Sky, Dear Dragon?

by Margaret Hillert
Illustrated by David Schimmell

NORWOOD HOUSE PRESS

DEAR CAREGIVER, The *Beginning-to-Read* series is a carefully written collection of classic readers you may remember from your own childhood. Each book features text comprised of common sight words to provide your child ample practice reading the words that appear most frequently in written text. The many additional details in the pictures enhance the story and offer the opportunity for you to help your child expand oral language and develop comprehension.

Begin by reading the story to your child, followed by letting him or her read familiar words and soon your child will be able to read the story independently. At each step of the way, be sure to praise your reader's efforts to build his or her confidence as an independent reader. Discuss the pictures and encourage your child to make connections between the story and his or her own life. At the end of the story, you will find reading activities and a word list that will help your child practice and strengthen beginning reading skills.

Above all, the most important part of the reading experience is to have fun and enjoy it!

Shannon Cannon

Shannon Cannon, Ph.D.
Literacy Consultant

Norwood House Press
For more information about Norwood House Press please visit our website at
www.norwoodhousepress.com or call 866-565-2900.

Text copyright ©2014 by Margaret Hillert. Illustrations and cover design copyright ©2014 by Norwood House Press, Inc. All rights reserved. No part of this book may be reproduced or utilized in any form or by any means without written permission from the publisher.

LIBRARY OF CONGRESS CATALOGING-IN-PUBLICATION DATA
    Hillert, Margaret.
      What's in the sky, dear dragon? / by Margaret Hillert ; illustrated by David Schimmell.
        pages cm. -- (A beginning-to-read book)
      Summary: "A boy and his pet dragon look at both the day and night skies.
    They learn about the sun, moon, animals, and airplanes that move through the
    sky. This title includes reading activities and a word list"-- Provided by publisher.
      ISBN 978-1-59953-580-7 (library edition : alk. paper)
      ISBN 978-1-60357-435-8 (ebook)
    [1. Sky--Fiction. 2. Dragons--Fiction.] I. Schimmell, David, illustrator.
    II. Title. III. Title: What is in the sky, dear dragon?
    PZ7.H558Wg 2013
    [E]--dc23

                        2012043566

Hardcover ISBN: 978-1-59953-580-7   Paperback ISBN: 978-1-60357-416-7

341—052021
Manufactured in the United States of America in North Mankato, Minnesota.

What's in the sky, Dear Dragon?
What's in the sky?
We can see some things at night.

Look up. Look up, Father.

Look way, way up.

I see something yellow.
It is pretty. It is big.
It gives us light.

Yes, Yes.
That is the moon.

I see some baby moons, too.

No, no.

They are not moons.

They are stars.

They give us light, too.

Are the little, little ones stars?

No.
They are fireflies.
You can get some to look at,
but then put them back.

Oh, look here.
The owl likes the night sky.

And look at this.
Oh, look at this!

What fun!
What fun!

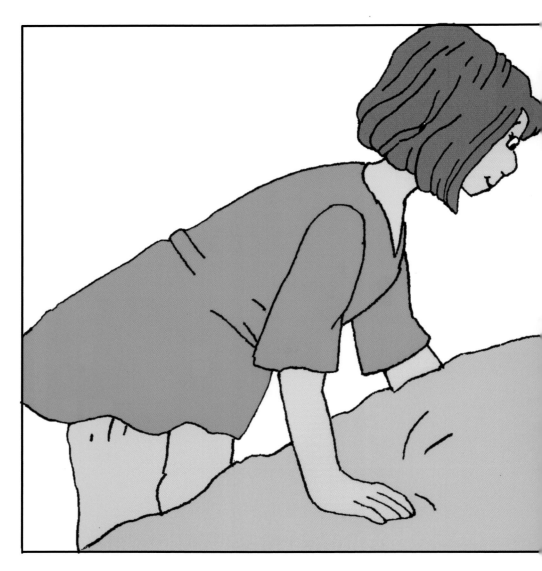

We will go to bed now.

When we wake up,
we will look at the day sky.

Now what we see is the sun.

The sun is big, big, big.
It gives us light, and helps things grow.

Clouds are in the sky.

Rain is in the sky, too.
Rain is in the dark clouds.

Sometimes the rain and sun
make a rainbow.
A pretty, pretty rainbow.

I see red and orange.
I see yellow and green and blue.

Birds are in the sky, too.
They are pretty too.
Look at them go.

An airplane is in the sky.
It is like a big bird.
It can go away, away, away.
We can go away with it.

We are in the airplane.
We will go, go, go.

You are here with me.
And I am here with you.
It is fun to be in the sky, Dear Dragon.

READING REINFORCEMENT

The following activities support the findings of the National Reading Panel that determined the most effective components for reading instruction are: Phonemic Awareness, Phonics, Vocabulary, Fluency, and Text Comprehension.

Phonemic Awareness: The /s/ sound

Substitution: Ask your child to say the following words without the /s/ sound:

sat - /s/ = at	spot - /s/ = pot	Sam - /s/ = am
sand - /s/ = and	she - /s/ = he	said - /s/ = aid
share - /s/ = hare	sin - /s/ = in	stop - /s/ = top

Phonics: The letter Ss

1. Demonstrate how to form the letters **S** and **s** for your child.

2. Have your child practice writing **S** and **s** at least three times each.

3. Ask your child to point to the words in the book that start with the letter **s**.

4. Write down the following words and ask your child to circle the letter **s** in each word:

see	sad	this	sky	say	was
set	clouds	shapes	miss	something	sip
ask	guess	star	said	house	sun

Vocabulary: Story Words

1. Write the following words on separate pieces of paper:

   sun   birds   stars   rainbow   airplane

2. Say the following sentences aloud and ask your child to point to the word that is described:

   - This gives us light in the day sky. (sun)
   - These animals have wings and can fly in the sky. (birds)
   - These twinkle and give off light in the night sky. (stars)
   - What colorful thing could you see in the sky after it rains? (rainbow)
   - What did the boy and Dear Dragon get on to go away in the sky? (airplane)

Fluency: Echo Reading

1. Reread the story to your child at least two more times while your child tracks the print by running a finger under the words as they are read. Ask your child to read the words he or she knows with you.

2. Reread the story, stopping after each sentence or page to allow your child to read (echo) what you have read. Repeat echo reading and let your child take the lead.

Text Comprehension: Discussion Time

1. Ask your child to retell the sequence of events in the story.

2. To check comprehension, ask your child the following questions:

   - What can you see in the sky at night?
   - What does the sun give to us?
   - Have you ever seen a rainbow? If so, where?
   - What other things can you see in the sky?

WORD LIST

What's in the Sky, Dear Dragon? uses the 85 words listed below.
The **12** words bolded below serve as an introduction to new vocabulary, while the other 73 are pre-primer. You may wish to write the words on index cards and use them to help your child build automatic word recognition. Regular practice with these words will enhance your child's fluency in reading connected text.

a	**dark**	**light**	rain	up
airplane	day	like(s)	**rainbow**	us
am	dear	little	red	
an	dragon	look		**wake**
and			see	way
are	Father	make	sky	we
at	**fireflies**	me	some	what
away	fun	**moon(s)**	something	what's
			sometimes	when
baby	get	**night**	**stars**	will
back	give(s)	no	sun	with
be	go	not		
bed	green	now	that	yellow
big	grow		the	yes
bird(s)		oh	them	you
blue	helps	ones	then	
but	here	orange	they	
		owl	things	
can	I		this	
clouds	in	pretty	to	
	is	put	too	
	it			

ABOUT THE AUTHOR Margaret Hillert has helped millions of children all over the world learn to read independently. She was a first grade teacher for 34 years and during that time started writing books that her students could both gain confidence in reading and enjoy. She wrote well over 100 books for children just learning to read. As a child, she enjoyed writing poetry and continued her poetic writings as an adult for both children and adults.

Photograph by Glenna Washburn

ABOUT THE ILLUSTRATOR David Schimmell served as a professional firefighter for 23 years before hanging up his boots and helmet to devote himself to working as an illustrator of children's books. David has happily created illustrations for the New Dear Dragon books as well as other artwork for educational and retail book projects. Born and raised in Evansville, Indiana, he lives there today with his wife and family.